CHOMPS
BIGGER BITES FOR BIGGER READERS!

The Twilight Ghost

Robby Green is new in Twilight.
He doesn't believe the local talk that the old
Children's Home is haunted by a vengeful ghost.
Then Robby sees the ghost and narrowly survives
a freak accident. Is the ghost trying
to kill him? Will he go through
with his dare to enter the old Home at night?

MORE CHOMPS TO SINK YOUR TEETH INTO!

THE BOY WHO WOULD LIVE FOREVER

Moya Simons

STELLA BY THE SEA

Ruth Starke

WALTER WANTS TO BE A WEREWOLF

Richard Harland

The Twilight Ghost

Beware the terror in the town of Twilight!

Colin Thiele

RUNNING PRESS
KIDS
PHILADELPHIA·LONDON

First published by Penguin Group (Australia),
a division of Pearson Australia Group Pty Ltd, 2004

Printed in China

9   8   7   6   5   4   3   2   1
Digit on the right indicates the number of this printing

Library of Congress Control Number: 2005935326

ISBN-13: 978-0-7624-2652-2
ISBN-10: 0-7624-2652-7

Original design by David Altheim and Miriam Rosenbloom, Penguin Group (Australia).
Additional design for this edition by Frances J. Soo Ping Chow

Typography: ITC Berkeley and MetaPlus

This book may be ordered by mail from the publisher.
Please include $2.50 for postage and handling.
But try your bookstore first!

This edition published by Running Press Kids, an imprint of
Running Press Book Publishers
125 South Twenty-Second Street
Philadelphia, Pennsylvania 19103-4399

Visit us on the web!
www.runningpress.com

Ages 8–12
Grades 3–6

Chapter 1

Have you ever seen a ghost? No? Well, I have. It's scary—more scary than anything in your whole life.

It all happened because we came to live in Twilight. It's a dump. They say there are two thousand people here. If you ask me, that's two thousand too many. I guess the ghosts are extra.

I don't know why anyone would want to live in Twilight. It's in the middle of a plain, with wheat fields all around as far as you can see. Flat and boring. And in August when we arrived it was so hot that you could fry an egg on the road.

So why did we come to live here? Because of

Dad, of course. He was sent out to manage the grain silos in the town. Concrete monsters they are, more than thirty yards high, like giant tombstones. You can see them rising up on the plain twenty miles away.

I sure didn't want to come here and I'm sure Mom didn't either, but she always makes the best of things. All my friends are in the city. If any of them ever saw Twilight they'd die of shock. But there was nowhere in the city where I could stay while I went to school, so I had to come out here.

The first thing we saw when we drove up to Twilight was the old Children's Home on the edge of the town. It's horrible. Most of the ghosts would have to be living in there, that's for sure.

It's a wreck—a huge two-story place like an old prison that goes on and on. The roof is rusting and the stairs are rotten. The doors are all gone, the windows are just rows of empty holes, and the broken gutters are hanging from the roof. Nobody has lived in it for fifty years. One of the beams near the front has fallen down because a terrific thunderbolt struck it during a storm. People say it was a sure sign that God was angry because of the things that happened in there.

We looked at it as we drove past in the car.

"It was called The Twilight Home," Dad said. "I guess that was a good name for it." He was being sarcastic.

"What was wrong with it?" I asked.

"The kids were treated like prisoners. Like slaves. So they say."

"What kids?"

"Orphans. Their parents were dead. They had no family. No friends. Nowhere to live."

Mom was sad. "No wonder the government shut the place down."

3

"It's supposed to be full of ghosts," Dad said. "Lots of people say they've seen them."

"Ghosts of people who died there?"

"Maybe. They say one of them looks like a girl of twelve or thirteen in a white dress." Dad glanced back at me. "About as old as you are, Robby."

My name is really Robert, but everyone calls me Robby. I haven't got a middle name. I'm just Robby Green. Some kids call me Greeny.

"I wonder how many stories are locked up in there," Mom said, "but will never be told."

Dad grunted. "Perhaps that's what the ghosts are trying to do."

A moment later, we arrived at the manager's house where we were going to live for the next few years. It was so close to the grain silos that they towered above it. We were like beetles on the ground in front of them.

"I'll have nightmares about those things," I

said. "One night they're going to crash down and squash us flat."

Mom was already on her way to the front door with the key. "For goodness sake stop complaining, Robby. The furniture van will be here in a minute and we have to get everything sorted out." She unlocked the door and pushed it open. "And school starts in a few weeks. Remember that."

"I can't wait," I said.

At that moment, a train loaded with wheat started to move away from the silos—a long caterpillar of cars hauled by a couple of big diesel locomotives that roared and strained when they reached full power. The ground trembled as the train gathered speed.

"*And* I won't be able to sleep," I called, "because of all the noise from the trains."

"Then you'll have to put a pillow over your head."

"Great. I'm glad everyone is so worried about me."

That night I stood at my bedroom window and looked out at the town. It was nothing but a disaster area with a ruin full of ghosts at one end and a heap of concrete silos at the other.

Chapter 2

The next morning I met Jim and Pippa Scott. They were twins just one day older than me. We were going to be in the same class at school, which was really cool. Their father worked at the grain silos with Dad and their mother knew Mom. Before long Jim was one of my best friends. He was crazy about stamp collecting. That didn't do anything for me, but I guess everyone likes to do something weird.

On the second day, Jim came over on his bike. He was wearing a big hat and he had a towel slung round his shoulders. "Want to come for a swim?" he called. "It's going to be hot."

"It's always hot. So where's the pool?"

He laughed. "There isn't a pool."

"Where, then?"

"Down in the creek. There's a waterhole. Deep and cool. It's a mile or two down the road."

"Okay. I'll get my stuff."

I was just coming out of our yard, when a big lump of a kid on a bike came skidding around the corner and almost ran over Jim.

"Out of the way," he shouted, and shot off down the street.

I stopped with a yell. "Who's that?"

Jim scoffed. "Slugger Sloan. He's a slob."

"A boxer?"

"Nuh. He couldn't box a dead fish."

"Then how did he get his name?"

"Made it up himself. He's a bighead. Pushes kids off their bikes and throws their bags in the gutter. Does bright things like that. He'll be in our class at school, so you'll see him every day."

"Great."

A second or two later another kid came past, riding like mad to catch up with Slugger.

"That's Red Carter," Jim said. "He's a wimp. Follows Slugger everywhere."

"He's got red hair?"

"Yeah. And big ears."

"Are there any more weird kids like that in Twilight?"

"Lots."

We rode off down the main road towards the creek. Halfway to the pool the railway line crossed the road. It was just our luck that a long wheat train rolled across in front of us. It seemed to go on and on forever while we had to wait in the heat.

"There was a terrible accident here a few years ago," Jim said. "A bus full of passengers was hit by a train. It was awful. Five people were killed. Karl Sloan said he could have guessed it."

"Who's Karl Sloan?"

"Slugger's big brother. He knows everything about the place."

"How old is he?"

"About twenty-five I think. He's rich. Drives a red Porsche. Don't ask me where his money comes from."

"Why did he say he could have guessed the accident was going to happen? Is the crossing dangerous?"

"No, because of the ghost."

"What ghost?"

"The one like a girl. Karl saw her right here at the crossing the night before the accident. He says it was a sure sign that something terrible was going to happen. It's the way ghosts take revenge on people for what happened years ago. If you

10

ever see the ghost of the girl in the white dress you should keep away from the place before you're killed."

I laughed. "That's crazy. Accidents can happen any time. Ghosts haven't got anything to do with it."

"This one has. Last year a kid called Ben Price drowned in the waterhole. He was a good swimmer. Karl tried to save him but it was too late."

"People drown every summer."

"The same ghost was down there the night before. Under the trees by the water."

I stared at him. "Honest?"

"Honest."

Just then, the last of the wheat trucks crossed in front of us and we rode on to the creek. I still didn't believe there were ghosts in Twilight that were waiting to take their revenge on living people.

As soon as we reached the waterhole we dived

in and swam around for a long time. The water felt as cool as a fridge after the heat of the road. Then we climbed out and sat on our towels under the trees.

There was one question I especially wanted to ask Jim, and this seemed the best time to ask it.

"Have you ever seen a ghost?" I said. "A real one?"

Jim took a while to answer. "Yeah. Once."

"You sure?"

"Sure I'm sure. But..."

"But what?"

"You can't see ghosts properly."

"What do you mean?"

"They're sort of fuzzy. Not clear and definite."

"Yours was like that?"

"Yeah. There were shadows and bits of moonlight. And the wind was shaking the trees and bushes so the ghost seemed to be moving about."

"Where was it?"

"By the old Home. Near the front."

"In the night?"

"Late. I was riding home after watching a video at Peter Border's place."

"Maybe you imagined it?"

"No way. It was there all right. Scared me cold. I rode home like crazy. Never looked back."

"Was it the girl in the white dress?"

"Sure was. She's the one most people see. Karl has seen her there lots of times."

"You haven't seen her again?"

"Nuh. Don't want to, either." Jim stood up and hung his towel on a branch. "Let's go for another swim. Then we'd better head home."

It was clear that he didn't want to say any more about ghosts.

Chapter 3

By the time we rode back to town we were hot and dusty again.

"I need a drink," Jim said. "You got any money?"

"Ten dollars."

"I'll owe you. Come into the deli and get something."

The deli was a crappy sort of place with dirty windows. The blowflies came in through the door but they didn't have the sense to find their way out again so they spent all day flying up and down rubbing their noses against the glass and looking at the world outside.

Mrs. Lockett ran the shop. She was a big woman with a loud voice. She didn't like kids, but she liked their money so she had to put up with them. She said they stole things behind her back, so she kept all the chocolate bars and chewing gum and stuff like that locked up in a big case behind the counter. You could see them there through the glass.

There were a few tables and chairs at one end of the deli where you could eat pie or a sandwich if you wanted to. An old man was sitting there when we walked in. He had a cup of tea and a plate with half-a-dozen crackers in front of him. One by one he dunked the crackers in the tea for a few seconds until they were soft and then lifted them up to his mouth as fast as he could before they fell to pieces.

While we were waiting to be served, Jim leaned over and whispered to me, "That's Eddy Benson.

He's eighty years old and he's lived in Twilight all his life. He knows everything about the place—the old Children's Home and things like that."

I paid for our drinks and we sat down nearby. Jim looked at Eddy. "Hello, Mr. Benson," he said.

Eddy stopped for a second to see who was speaking. "Ah, hi, Jimmy."

"This is my friend Robby Green," Jim said.

Eddy stopped dunking crackers and eyed me. "You're new here are you boy?"

"Yes. Dad's come to manage the silos."

Eddy nodded. "Yeah. I heard."

We were quiet for a while. Jim slurped his drink and I pocketed the change I had in my hand.

"I've been telling Robby about the old Home," Jim said. "About the ghosts and that."

Eddy dunked the last of his crackers, but didn't answer.

"It was a rotten place wasn't it? In the old days?" Jim was trying hard to get Eddy to tell some of his stories. "You'd be about the only guy left in Twilight who still knows about it."

Eddy nodded slowly. "I know."

"You even went inside sometimes and saw the kids, didn't you?"

He nodded again. "Saw lots of things."

"What sort of things?"

Eddy took a long time to think about it. "The kids were bashed, you know. And starved. I saw 'em when I took stuff to the kitchen. Groceries and that. On my bike. I was only sixteen then and I was workin' in Simpson's shop." He thought again for a while. "There was a nice girl in a white dress. About fourteen she was. Down on her knees, scrubbin' and scrubbin' the floor and bein' yelled at and pushed about. She's a ghost now."

17

"You've seen her, haven't you?" Jim said. "Her ghost, I mean."

"Not as often as Karl Sloan. He sees her all the time. By the old Home. He can tell you all about it."

Eddy finished his tea and crackers and stood up. "Got to go," he said. "If you want to know more, just ask Karl."

Chapter 4

On Saturday morning, Jim came over and called out from the street. "Baseball's on today. Up for a game?"

I answered from the porch. "Sure."

"A guy called Barry Burke is arranging it."

"Who plays?"

"Some of the kids from school and a few guys from the town. Pip plays too, and a couple of other girls."

I had seen Pippa in the backyard, throwing a ball like a rocket, so I guessed she'd be a good player. "Who're the captains of the teams?" I asked.

"Slugger Sloan and me."

"Slugger?"

"Yeah, but don't worry. I'll see that Barry puts you on my team."

I pointed to the diamond not far from the silos. "We play over there?"

Jim laughed. "No way. The town team uses that."

"Where do we play?"

"Over in Benson's field. Near the old Home."

I couldn't help being smart. "Do the ghosts play too?"

He grinned. "Not in the daytime."

"Maybe after dark?"

"Sure."

"Are they supposed to come out of the air?"

Jim shrugged. "Don't ask me. Out of their graves. Or from under the floor."

"You believe that?"

"Karl Sloan does. If you want to know more go and talk to him. He knows everything."

I rode over to Benson's field, where Barry Burke was arranging the players in the teams.

Jim took me over to meet him. "This is Robby Green," he said.

Barry shook my hand. "Hi Robby. Do you play infield or outfield?"

"A bit of both I guess." I didn't want to sound like a bighead.

"Okay. You're on Jim's team. You'll be playing against Slugger's crowd."

I rolled my eyes and Barry smiled. "Actually Slugger can hit the ball. You'll soon find out."

It was a good game. Jim won the toss and batted first. He and a kid called Darren Baker opened the inning for us and they each scored a run. But then the next two batters were both struck out and our inning fell to pieces. I walked, Pippa struck out, and we finished with two runs.

When Slugger's team went in to bat they struck

out twice, but then Slugger and Red Carter came up to bat. Barry was right about Slugger. He lashed out at the ball and sent it sizzling to the fence. He kept jeering at us the whole time, yelling and dancing around the bases whenever he passed one of us. Barry told him to calm down a couple of times, but it didn't make any difference. Slugger couldn't help being unbearable.

Later in the game, when his team only needed one run to win he ended the game with a tremendous home run. He hit the ball square in the sweet spot of the bat and sent it flying high over the wire fence that separated Benson's field from the old Home. It bounced twice and then rolled on for another five or six yards before stopping right in front of the entrance.

I was deep in center field, so it was my job to get it. By now it was late in the afternoon. Clouds were covering the sun and everything was in shadow. I crawled through the fence and ran across the open space in front of the Home. While I was bending down to pick up the ball I turned my head and looked right into the big opening that used to be the main entrance. I could just see a few dim shapes far inside. There was a staircase with a curving banister rail that had partly fallen down. Some of the carved wooden supports that were supposed to hold it up had broken loose and were leaning at crooked angles.

I only had time for a quick look into the gloom, but it gave me the creeps. A stream of cold air was coming out of it, and somewhere inside a bit of loose iron or wood was scraping backwards and forwards. It sounded like someone scratching a message or trying to get out of a locked room. I looked away quickly, picked up the ball, and threw it back as hard as I could.

Slugger was carrying on more than ever to celebrate his victory, dancing about and waving his arms in the air as though he had just won the World Series. "We slaughtered you," he yelled. He was especially full of himself because of his big home run that had won the game.

Darren Baker was sick of him. "Shut up, Slugger," he called. "Why don't you go and sit on something sharp."

Everyone laughed, but it didn't stop Slugger. "You're a bunch of wimps," he crowed.

"We'll play you again next week," Jim said, "and we'll knock the socks off you."

"We sure will," I added. I was feeling down because I didn't get a hit, and I'd had to chase Slugger's home run.

Slugger turned and gave me a blast. "Next week I'll belt the ball right into the old Home and then you'll be too scared to go in and get it."

He was really getting up my nose with his stupid comments. "Huh," I shouted. "I'd go in any time you like."

Barry Burke decided to put an end to it all. "Can it, you guys," he said. "Time to go. See that you put away all the gear."

Jim came over to me while we were packing up. "Sorry about that chase you had. It's the first time I've seen a ball go that far. Just as well you didn't have to go right inside."

I was still angry. "If Slugger carries on like that next week, I'll go right inside just to shut him up."

"I wouldn't if I was you. Better watch what you say."

Barry Burke was standing nearby. "That's right," he said. "It's not the sort of place to mess about in. Keep away from it."

It sounded as though he was trying to give me a warning.

Chapter 5

"You're a mobile disaster. You don't think. You go around all day with your brain switched off, looking for accidents." Dad was blasting me full on and Mom was agreeing with him.

It was all because I'd wrecked my bike. I was riding down the street with Jim when it happened. We were mucking about, zigzagging, and hopping up and down over the concrete gutter. I was in the lead when I accidentally missed the jump. My front wheel hit the curb as if I'd run into a low brick wall and I went flying over the handlebars onto the sidewalk. I got up groggily. Little beads of blood were starting to dot a rash on my knee.

Jim skidded to a stop beside me. "You okay?"

"I hope."

He pointed to the blood. "You'll have to put something on that."

My bike was a wreck. The front wheel was buckled into a weird loop and the handlebars were twisted sideways.

"Just look at it," I said. "It's a heap of junk."

"Take it down to Simpson's workshop," Jim suggested. "Sam Simpson can fix anything."

I limped down to the workshop, dragging the bike after me.

Sam came out and stood looking at it. "Whoa, whoa," he said. "Hit something?"

"Yeah. Can you fix it, please?"

Sam nodded. "I think. But it'll take a day or two."

I dreaded asking the next question. "How much will it cost?"

"About a hundred bucks."

I felt sick to my stomach. "A hundred bucks?"

"Yeah. And that's cheap."

There wasn't anything I could do about it, but I knew there would be an awful explosion when Mom and Dad found out.

Sam looked at the blood on my knee. "Better go home and patch that." He hauled the bike into the workshop. "I'll see what I can do. Come back in a couple of days."

As soon as Mom saw the blood she wanted to know what had happened, and when I mentioned the hundred dollars she went bananas. "For heaven's sake, try to take care of your things for a change. We can't afford a hundred dollars every time you decide to wreck something. You'll have to pay for it yourself."

"But I haven't got a hundred dollars."

"Then you'll have to earn it."

That was when Dad came in. He carried on for ten minutes without stopping for breath. But in the end his throat went dry and he had to go to the fridge to get a drink. While he was there I took my chance and snuck off to my room. I looked out miserably through the window. I didn't have any money, so what would happen to me if Mom and Dad refused to pay Sam Simpson? I'd probably be arrested.

On Saturday morning I had to walk all the way to Benson's field for the baseball game, because Sam hadn't finished fixing my bike. By the time I got there I was hot and tired, and when the game started everything went wrong. Jim and Darren were the only ones on our team to get hits. I was struck out three times, and the rest made less than three runs between them.

When Slugger's team went in to bat I dropped a

simple catch and misfielded three or four times. Slugger crowed more than ever. He jeered and shouted, waving his bat in the air and dancing about on home plate whenever he scored. He purposely tried to hit the ball, so that I had to run over to the old Home to get it.

"What are you doing over there again, Greeny?" he yelled. "Karl says the white ghost was there again last night. She's waiting to get you."

His team won the game so easily that it was a joke. By the time it ended I was fed up and furious. Slugger noticed it and so he kept on needling me. "You're taking a risk, Greeny, hanging around the Home like that. They'll get you any time now."

It made me madder than ever. "Ah, shut up," I snapped. "It's just an empty old dump. I'd go in there any time."

"Yeah?" he sneered. "Not when it's dark, you wouldn't."

"Yes, I would."

The words slipped out before I could stop them. My brain seemed to be switched off, but my mouth went on talking.

Slugger crowed. "You'd never have the guts."

"Yes, I would."

"You'd be scared out of your mind."

I was trapped. I couldn't chicken out now, or he'd call me a wimp in front of all the other kids and keep on trashing me for the rest of my life.

"Bet you a hundred dollars you wouldn't do it."

I tried to change tack. "Huh, where would you get a hundred dollars?"

"I've got it. And if I didn't, I'd get it from Karl." Karl always drove about in his Porsche and seemed to have plenty of money.

"Where would he get it from?"

"He's got lots, don't worry."

"I'd like to know."

Slugger came back to the bet. "A hundred dollars. No, make it two hundred. Are you on, or are you just a windy little fart?"

If only I had kept my mouth shut. I knew I'd painted myself into a corner. Slugger kept pushing me. "You're scared, aren't you? You're scared stiff."

"No, I'm not." It was hopeless. All I could do was to keep on saying, "No I'm not, no I'm not, no I'm not," like a little kid.

"Right," Slugger said. "The bet's on. Has to be between ten o'clock and four the next morning. Any time from now until next Saturday." He was enjoying himself, making up the rules as he went along. "And you have to go right in, not just a couple of steps near the entrance. Tell you what, you have to bring back one of those bits of wood that hold up the banister rail on the steps in there. That'll prove it. Red and me will be waiting for you."

I was so terrified that I couldn't answer properly. Slugger kept on at me. "You've got a week. If you haven't done it by Saturday you owe me two hundred dollars. You better have it ready. Just let me know which night you pick."

I wanted to walk away, but Slugger's threat froze my legs. The thought that I would have to find two hundred dollars if I chickened out was only just entering my head. Where would I find two hundred dollars? I already owed Sam Simpson a hundred. It would take forever to save that much, but Slugger would want the money right away. I couldn't bear to think of the things he would get Karl to do to me if I didn't pay up on time.

Jim made things worse. "You've got rocks in your head," he hissed as we walked off. "Why the heck did you do it?"

"It just slipped out. Slugger made me so mad that I didn't think."

Jim pointed at the Home. "You're going to walk in there after dark? All by yourself? You're a loony."

"Yeah, yeah, yeah."

"Either that, or you pay Slugger two hundred dollars."

"I haven't got two hundred dollars."

"He'll bash you up if you don't."

I didn't answer. There was a knot in my stomach and my blood felt cold. I wondered if I should run away and hide somewhere. Or maybe have an accident. If I had to lie in the hospital for a week then I couldn't carry out the bet. But that was a hopeless idea. Slugger would be waiting for me as soon as I came out. Maybe Karl, too.

I groaned. "God, what a mess."

"You'll have to tell your mom and dad. Maybe

they'll lend you the money."

My knees went weak at the thought. "Dad'll go mad," I said. "I'm in enough trouble with him already—over my bike."

We walked silently side by side. After a while I turned to Jim. "Listen. What do you say we both go in there? It wouldn't be so bad with two of us."

Jim laughed. "No way."

"Please?"

"No."

"Just this once?"

"It's your problem. You got yourself sucked into it. You have to get yourself out of it."

"Thanks," I said. "Thanks a lot."

Chapter 6

When I got home I must have looked as sick as I felt because Mom eyed me as soon as I walked in. "Are you all right?" she asked.

"I feel a bit off."

"Then you'd better have some dinner and go to bed early."

"Yeah, I think I will."

I was glad to hide in my room. There was no way I could tell Mom and Dad about the bet. They'd go ballistic. I couldn't sleep. The room was hot, and the awful mess I was in kept squirming about in my head.

At about eleven o'clock I got up and went to

the kitchen to get a cold drink from the fridge. I thought it might calm me down, but it didn't help. I still kept tossing and turning on my bed, thinking about the bet and the ghost in the Home, over and over and over.

It must have been near midnight when I happened to turn my head towards the window and froze. Something was outside watching me. It was a filmy shape, a figure like a girl in a white dress. It was hard to see it clearly because branches and twigs from a tree in the garden were moving in the breeze and throwing shadows across the window. But something was out there alright, looking at me through the glass. I was more scared than I've ever been in my life. I knew it was the ghost.

I looked again and I thought it moved forward as though it wanted to come in through the window. That did it. I wanted to scream but I couldn't. My tongue seemed to be jammed in my mouth. I grabbed the sheet and pulled it over my head. I was shivering. I could feel my heart thumping. I knew that ghosts could go through walls. At any minute it would be in my room.

I didn't know what to do. If I woke Mom and Dad, yelling ghost, ghost, they'd think I'd lost my marbles. Dad had to go to work early so he'd be in a rage if I shook him awake in the middle of the night.

I don't know how long I kept lying with my head buried under the bedclothes. It might have been ten seconds or ten minutes. But at last, when nothing else happened, I carefully lifted one corner of the sheet and took a quick look at the window. There was nothing out there. I sat up slowly and looked long and hard. Nothing. Just the moving shadows of the branches and the soft sound of the breeze outside.

I started to calm down. My heart wasn't beating

so fast any more and the cold feeling in my chest started to fade away. I waited and waited. Finally I got out of bed, tiptoed over to the window, and looked outside. Everything was normal—just the shape of the tree, the patches of moonlight and shadow, and the big bulk of the silos beyond the house. I stood at the window for a long time but I knew there was nothing I could do except go back to bed.

I couldn't sleep. My head was swimming so much that in the end I didn't know whether I'd seen a ghost at all.

In the morning when I tottered into the kitchen for breakfast, Mom gazed at me sharply. "Not feeling any better?"

"No, still a bit off."

"Then you'd better take it easy today. School starts in a week. You'll need to be well by then."

The thought of school was the last straw. I had

more than enough on my mind with a wrecked bike, no money, a lunatic bet, and a ghost at my window.

"I'll go and see Jim," I said. "I think we'll go for a swim."

Jim was out on the porch and came down to meet me. "You look awful," he said. "Have you seen a ghost?"

It was unbelievable. People shouldn't make sick jokes like that. But when I told him about the figure at the window he goggled. "That's exactly like the one I saw," he said. "It would have to be the same one."

"It wasn't very plain, was it—the one you saw?"

"Nuh. It was sort of fuzzy."

"With moonlight and shadows and that?"

"Yeah."

"Mine was like that too."

"It was the same one for sure."

40

I thought for a while. The sunshine was warm and the morning was bright and clear. The world around us was so different from the shadows and gloom of the night before that it was hard to imagine ghosts at all.

"The thing you saw," I said. "It really was a ghost, wasn't it? It wasn't something else that just looked like one. Maybe we both just thought we saw a ghost."

"Nuh."

"But we didn't check it out, did we?"

"What d'you mean?"

"If I'd gone right up to the window, there mightn't have been a ghost there at all. It might have been reflections and moonlight and stuff."

"Couldn't be."

"Maybe people are too scared to have a good look. They run away, or cover their heads like I did, but if they stayed they might find out that it's

41

all light and air and moonshine."

"What about the ones that Eddie and Karl and everyone else see all the time?"

"But they haven't been really close to them, have they? Someone ought to go right up to the ghost and touch it."

Jim drew back. "If you did that you'd be dead."

We were silent again until Jim changed the subject. "Forget about ghosts," he said. "Let's get our stuff and go for a swim."

Chapter 7

When I met Jim one morning, a day or two later, he looked miserable.

"What's up?" I asked. "Did the dog eat your breakfast?"

He looked at me sadly. "I need a hundred dollars."

I almost laughed. "So do I. What d'you want it for?"

"Stamps."

I couldn't believe it. Stamps? It took a while for me to remember that he was crazy about stamp collecting.

"I've got the chance to get a real bargain but I

haven't got enough money to pay for it."

"What is it?"

"An excellent album, full of good stuff."

"Where from?"

"Mike Lee. He's selling it because he needs the money. He only wants two hundred dollars for it. It's worth twice as much."

"Then you need two hundred, not one hundred."

"I've got a hundred saved up. I only need another hundred."

"What about your mom and dad? Can't they lend it to you?"

"No. They say they spent a lot of money on Christmas presents for Pip and me and they can't afford any more." Jim had a hangdog look. "I'd do anything to get that album. I'll never get another chance like it."

That was when I had a really smart idea. "Tell you what," I said slyly. "Come with me into the old

Home and we'll share the money from Slugger's bet. A hundred dollars each. What do you say?"

"I'm not going in there after dark."

"But it would fix everything for both of us."

"There are real ghosts in there."

"We'd run. We'd be in and out in a wink."

"Yeah?"

"We'd make two hundred dollars in thirty seconds. Next morning you'd have your stamps."

Jim started to waver. "D'you think we could do it?"

"Easy. And we'd stick it to Slugger at the same time. He'd be as mad as a cut snake."

Jim half smiled. "Yeah, he would."

"Be worth doing it just for that."

It took a few more minutes to persuade Jim, but in the end he agreed—even though he said he was scared out of his mind.

"I've been thinking," I said. "Mom and Dad

45

have to go out on Friday night, so I'll be home on my own. We could do it then. You could say you were coming over to stay at my place."

"Yeah. Friday night would be best."

"I'll tell Slugger. He says he and Red Carter are going to watch from Benson's field to make sure I do it. I have to go in through the front and come out again with one of those wooden pegs that hold up the banister rail on the stairs. And it has to be later than ten o'clock."

"Ten o'clock would be better than midnight. Maybe the ghosts wouldn't be out yet."

"Everyone says they come out as soon as it's dark."

"What if we meet one?"

"We run." It was such an awful thought that we both shuddered.

"There's one more thing," Jim said. "Slugger made the bet with you, so he'd want you to do it on your own, wouldn't he? He might pull out if he knows we're doing it together."

"I've thought of that. You'll have to hide near the entrance where they can't see you. Then you can join me when I walk in."

"We'll have flashlights, won't we?"

"Sure. Big ones."

Jim took a deep breath. "So it's all settled?"

"Yeah. I'll let Slugger know."

"What if he won't pay up? It would be awful if we went into that place and still didn't get the money."

"He'll pay up all right. All the other guys in the team know about the bet. They'd call him a creep for the rest of his life if he pulled out. He couldn't bear that."

"It's settled then," Jim said for the second time. "Ten o'clock, Friday."

"Yeah, ten o'clock."

We were both in a panic. I was just going to walk off when a police car with three officers in it drove up and stopped in front of Mrs. Lockett's deli. The driver was Sergeant Hoff who was in charge of the Twilight police station, but the other two were strangers. The three of them got out and walked straight into the shop.

"What do they want?" I said. "Are they going to arrest Mrs. Lockett for charging too much for her potato chips?"

Jim laughed. "Dad says they've been snooping around for a couple of days."

"Doing what?"

"Asking questions."

"What's new about that? Maybe they're trying to find out whether the white ghost has been causing any more accidents in Twilight."

"No. They think someone in Twilight is selling drugs."

Chapter 8

That night, for the second time in a row, I couldn't sleep. My nerves were all wound up, and my mind was full of pictures of the old Home. I could see Jim and me walking into that awful place in the dark. Ghosts were waiting to come out from hidden corners everywhere.

I was still in bed when the sun came up. Mom and Dad were talking in the kitchen while they were having breakfast. Then Dad's footsteps thumped across the floor, the door opened and shut, and I knew he was on his way to work at the silos.

I heard a loaded wheat train in the distance. It was coming down from Horseshoe Creek or some other town further out. The noise got louder and louder as it neared Twilight because the line passed within a few yards of our silos and then curved away across the highway on its way to the coast. Soon it was so close that the ground trembled.

And just when it seemed to be right beside us there was an incredible crash like an exploding bomb, and then another and another and another.

For a second or two I didn't know what had happened. The air seemed to be torn apart by the most hideous din—grinding shrieks and squeals and the awful sound of iron and steel being wrenched and twisted and ripped to pieces. A second later I guessed the truth. The train had left the line.

I leaped out of bed in my pajamas and almost collided with Mom as we both rushed outside. The sight left us speechless. Fifty-ton wagons had been flung about wildly; some heaped on top of each other like earthquake wreckage three stories high.

Others were lying at weird angles, on their sides, upside down, or even facing backwards. Many had their wheels wrenched off and their sides torn open, with wheat pouring out of the gashes like golden waterfalls. But there was an even more frightening sight ahead. Two of the heavy wagons had slammed into the bottom of the nearest silo and punched a big hole in the concrete. The awful noise still echoed over the town and dust from the dry ground was swirling up in brown clouds.

Mom started to run forward, crying out for Dad. I followed her but then I looked up at the nearest silo and stopped. It was tilted at an angle like the Leaning Tower of Pisa.

"Stop!" I yelled. "Stop! Stop! Look at the silo!"

We turned and ran off to the right, heading for shelter behind the office building at the railway station. We were only just in time. A second later the silo started to topple, slowly at first like a movie scene in slow motion, but then faster and faster until it hit the ground with a roar. It shattered into a thousand pieces, hurling bits in all directions like shrapnel. A big chunk the size of a boulder broke away and skidded forward into the wall of my bedroom, sending up a shower of broken bricks, timber, and glass.

Mom's face was as white as paper. "Oh, my God!" she kept saying. "Oh, my God!"

At last there was silence. We heard voices calling as the two drivers came hurrying towards us. Amazingly they weren't hurt. Both of the big locomotives were still standing on the line. Then Dad and Mr. Scott came running around the far end of the wreckage, shouting to see if we were okay. At the same time, Mrs. Scott, Jim, and Pippa rushed up, terrified that some of the men had been killed. Luckily everyone was safe, even though the drivers were shaking from shock.

"She jumped the line," one of them kept saying. "She jumped the line."

Dad pushed back the hat on his head. "The rails must have buckled," he answered. "It's been as hot as a furnace for weeks."

Jim and I stood staring at what was left of my bedroom. "If you'd been in bed," Jim said, "You'd be dead now."

The thought shook me. "I just got out in time."

Jim had a queer look in his eyes. "It was the white ghost that watched you through your window," he said slowly. "She tried to wipe you out, just like the bus people and Ben Price at the creek."

I didn't answer. I was still shaking from the awful noise of the crash, and the sight of the wreckage lying all around. I had often dreamed that the silos were crashing down on our house. Now it had happened right in front of me.

Chapter 9

That night I stayed at Jim's house because my own bedroom was a wreck. I couldn't sleep. Jim's comment about the ghost terrified me. If it really was trying to kill me, then what was going to happen when we went into the old Home?

I was so scared that I wanted to chicken out of the whole deal, but Jim said we couldn't do that. Slugger would jeer at us for the rest of our lives, and in any case we both needed the money. So we had to go ahead with it. I trembled more than ever at the thought. I was sure the ghost would be waiting for us as soon as we walked in through the front entrance.

When I arrived at the Home on Friday night, Slugger and Red were waiting near Benson's fence.

"Didn't think you'd turn up," Slugger said. He sounded disappointed to see me.

"You'd better have your money ready," I answered. "I'll be back in a minute to collect it." I tried to sound carefree, but my voice was trembling.

Slugger sneered. "When you come running out out of there you'll need a new pair of pants. And if you're not back in ten minutes we'll know you're dead."

I felt dizzy. My heart was thumping and the flashlight in my hand was shaking so much that Slugger noticed it.

"Hang onto that light, Greeny," he jeered. "If you drop it you'll be gone. Things in there come out of the dark like lightning."

I could see what Slugger was up to. He was trying to scare me so much that I'd back out of the bet. It made me mad. "Just shut up," I snapped and walked straight off into the Home.

Although the night was dark, there was just a haze of moonlight coming through the clouds. It made the place spookier than ever. Patches of gloomy shadow were mixed with the dark. I swung the light of the flashlight nervously from side to side as I walked in. The entrance was like an enormous mouth swallowing me up. My nerves were so taut that Jim almost sent me running when he slipped from the darkness to join me.

"Hi," he whispered.

I stepped back with a shock. "Oh!"

"You scared?"

"Dead scared."

"Me too."

I was glad Jim had still turned up. At least there were two of us to walk in together.

The floor was littered with rubble—bits of stone, broken bricks, and old pieces of wood—so we had to watch where we walked. In places the floorboards were rotten and dangerous. We had only gone a few yards when Jim twisted his ankle on a chunk of stone and winced. "Ouch!"

"Shhhh. Don't make a noise," I said.

"I've hurt my foot."

"Forget it. We have to keep going."

We were whispering, scared that something might be listening to us. There were dark openings on either side—black hollows that led to rooms and corridors and spaces far inside. The walls beside us rose up to the second floor like a prison. Faint squares of moonlight marked out the holes where the windows used to be.

"God, this is an awful place," Jim whispered.

Suddenly a strange shape loomed out of the dark. For a second it seemed to be moving towards us and we lurched back terrified. "Ugggh." But it was only a big window frame that had crashed down from above and was leaning crookedly against the wall.

"W…Watch out," I whispered.

We went on, more frightened at every step, until at last the outline of the old staircase showed up ahead. "Nearly there," I whispered.

Jim was limping. "Just as well. My ankle is swelling up. I can feel it."

When we reached the bottom of the stairs we shone our flashlights up the high curve of the banister rail to the second floor. Long ago, the big stairway would have been grand to look at, but now it was broken and decayed. I handed my flashlight to Jim. "Here, shine both lights on the stairs while I try to pull out one of the supports."

"They sure look like a row of baseball bats," Jim said.

"Some bats."

"Be careful. The whole thing's rotten."

I held on to the banister rail and leaned forward to get a good grip on the nearest peg holding it up. Although it was loose, it wouldn't come out no matter how hard I tugged.

"Try the next one," Jim whispered. "It might be easier."

I glanced up the stairs at the long line of supports. "It might too."

And then I saw it.

It was looking down at us from the top of the stairs—a figure like a girl in a filmy white dress. She didn't seem to be standing on the landing at all, but in the air above it.

It was the ghost.

I froze. Jim made a gurgling noise and jerked back. We didn't take a second look. All we wanted to do was get out of the place. Nothing else mattered—not the bet, not the stamps, not the bike, nothing but the urge to run, run, run, back to the real world outside.

It all happened in a flash. As I sprang back from the stairs I didn't even know that I was still gripping the second wooden support from the underside of the banister rail. It came away and stayed in my hand as though my fingers were glued to it.

Then everything exploded. A long piece of the heavy banister rail broke away altogether and came crashing down within inches of our heads. It brought a shower of supports with it, and part of the stairs as well. Then, in the middle of the din and swirling dust, the weight of the falling stairs was so great that they crashed right through the floor at our feet and a strange burst of light came up out of the hole in front of us. A hole which widened as the boards we were standing on suddenly gave way and pitched us down into the hollow below.

In that awful second I was sure that everything Jim had said about the ghost was true. It was going to kill us.

Chapter 10

It took a while for me to crawl out of the chaos. I wasn't hurt, but I was worried about Jim. "Are you okay?" I called.

"I think." His voice sounded shaky. "But I've got a lump on my head."

We both looked around. We were in a cellar of some kind, or an underground storage room. But it wasn't a dirty ruin like the rest of the Home. It looked clean and modern, a bit like a science lab. There were shelves with flasks and bottles, some of them smashed by the falling beams, as well as cans of chemicals, plastic bins and buckets, cardboard boxes, packets of pills, and other odds and ends. An electric light was shining from a socket on the wall, so there must have been a power cable somewhere.

"What the . . . ?" Jim said under his breath.

I managed to sit up. "What is this place?"

But then the memories of the last few seconds came flooding back into my head. "It was a ghost, wasn't it?" I said. "A real ghost?"

"Sure it was a ghost."

"The same one as always?"

"Yeah, the same one."

"Then let's get out of here. Fast."

"How?"

"Pile up some of the junk so we can climb out."

We were whispering to each other, afraid that the ghost was still watching and listening.

We started to pull out some of the biggest pieces of wood to try to build some sort of ramp.

Suddenly Jim stopped with a gasp. "Look!" he hissed. "Look! Look!"

I stared. A body was lying half covered by pieces of timber. It was a man, unconscious or dead. We bent down and cleared away the rubble around him until we were able to see him clearly. We were shocked. It was Karl Sloan.

"Is he alive?" Jim whispered.

I leaned forward and looked carefully. I didn't know how to check a person's pulse, but I could see that Karl's chest was moving slowly up and down. "He's still breathing," I said.

Jim eyed the body. "What are we going to do? We can't get him out of here on our own. We could never lift him."

"How did he get in here?"

"Down those steps I guess." There was a steep little staircase in the corner that must have led up through a trapdoor to the floor above.

"I think this was a cellar in the old days—for storing food and stuff. Now Karl is using it as a lab."

We both looked at Karl's unconscious body. "We'll have to get help," Jim said. "Otherwise he might die."

We managed to scramble out of the cellar over the pile of broken beams. I stood looking about. There was no sign of the ghost. Our flashlights had disappeared in the wreckage somewhere, but there was enough light to see vaguely. Let's go straight ahead," Jim suggested. "There's an opening at the other end. I've seen it."

He was right. After a minute or two we could see faint moonlight ahead, and we hurried towards it without ever looking back. As soon as we were out in the open air, we headed for Dr. Mitchell's place as fast as we could, even though Jim was limping like an old man.

"Slugger and Red will still be waiting for you at the front entrance," Jim said. "By now they'll think they're never going to see you again."

"Well, I sure don't want to see them again. Not just now."

"Because you haven't got anything to show him—from the banister."

"I'll get it when we go back. There are dozens of pieces lying around in there now."

By the time we reached Dr. Mitchell's house we were both out of breath. He was used to sudden emergencies in the night, so he wasn't alarmed when we came hammering on the door.

"Okay," he said, when we had told him our story, "I'll come right away. And I'll call the police."

Sergeant Hoff was about to get into his pajamas, but he was just as used to strange disasters as Dr. Mitchell. "Alright," he said when he arrived. "Show me."

We all travelled together in the police car. The sergeant called the ambulance as we drove along in case it was needed right away. I wondered what Slugger would think if he saw it hurrying towards the back of the Home. He'd be sure that I must've been zapped by a ghost and left for dead.

Sergeant Hoff carried a huge electric lamp with a beam like a searchlight. When he reached the edge of the cellar he stood in amazement looking down at Karl and the wreckage around him—the bottles, flasks, boxes, broken glass, and all the other stuff.

"I don't believe it," he said, moving the light from side to side, "I just don't believe it."

"A secret drug factory," Dr. Mitchell said.

"Yes, right under our noses. And all the time we couldn't work out where the stuff was coming from."

"This is a perfect hiding place."

"Yes, guarded by a ghost to frighten people away."

The doctor picked up his medical bag. "I must go down and see how he is." He swung himself down expertly and examined Karl for some time.

"How is he?" the sergeant called.

"No broken bones as far as I can tell. But fairly severe concussion. Must have been hit on the head when these two young fellows brought the roof down on top of him. We'll have to get him to the hospital."

Luckily two paramedics came hurrying up just then. It was a tricky job for them to strap Karl on a stretcher and haul him out of the cellar, but they managed it after a while and carried him back to the ambulance.

Sergeant Hoff turned to Jim and me. "And now perhaps I'd better take you two ghost busters home."

I bent down and picked up one of the supports from the broken banister rail. "Do you mind if I take this with me?"

He eyed me oddly. "That would really be stolen property. Why do you want a thing like that?"

I was embarrassed. "Well, it's a fairly complicated story."

The next day the news broke like a bombshell. Karl was charged with making and selling drugs. He would almost certainly be sent to jail.

Sergeant Hoff and a special squad of police from the city spent two days in the old cellar at the Home, gathering everything carefully and taking it away. All the people in Twilight were stunned. Nobody had ever suspected that such a thing could happen in the town. Our photos were printed on the front page of the newspapers and we were interviewed for radio and television right in the middle of the old Home. The camera crews went through the whole place, filming every-where. They laughed and joked while they went about it. "If there were ever any ghosts in here they've all gone now—over the hills and far away."

At first Mom and Dad were mad at us. Dad said it was a disgusting and sneaky thing to do, to go into a place like the Home in the middle of the night without telling them. But they calmed down after a while, especially when the police praised us for what we did.

A day or two later, Sergeant Hoff asked us to come to the police station. We were scared that we were going to be in trouble for damaging the Home or stealing things from it. But he just said he had something to show us. When he brought it out it looked like a heap of junk—a framework of wood with some white cloth draped over it.

"What's it supposed to be?" Jim asked.

Sergeant Hoff chuckled. "It's a ghost."

"A what?"

"A ghost. Specially made."

We caught on at last. "Did Karl make it?"

"He surely did. And then he used it in different places to frighten people—to stop them from going into the Home and finding out what he was up to."

"So we were scared by a bit of white rag?"

"Yes, but you were brave enough to go into the old Home after dark. You solved the puzzle of the ghost and you found Karl's secret den, even though you did it by accident. Now there'll never be any more ghosts in Twilight."

"But what about the accidents the ghost caused," Jim said. "The train crash, the bus disaster, and things like that?"

Sergeant Hoff scoffed. "They were stories Karl made up. His 'ghost' had nothing to do with accidents. The railway lines simply buckled in the heat, the bus driver didn't see the train. Accidents happen. They're not caused by ghosts."

He looked at us with a big smile. "And there's something more. A reward of a thousand dollars was on offer to anyone who could tell the police where the drugs were coming from. I've recommended that you should get it. Five hundred dollars each."

Jim and I gaped with our eyes and mouths wide open. We were speechless. Now we wouldn't have to worry about the bet any more. Slugger could keep his money, Jim could buy the stamp album, I could pay Sam Simpson for fixing my bike. And we'd still have money left over.

Suddenly Twilight wasn't such a bad place after all.

Chapter 11

On the following Friday night, Dad had to go out to Horseshoe Creek to see a farmer called Tom Judd about disease in his wheat.

"Want to come for a drive?" he said.

A trip out into that boring country was no big deal, but for once Dad seemed to want me to come with him to keep him company so I said okay.

When we got there he and Mr. Judd talked forever. After that Mrs. Judd asked us to stay for supper, so it was late by the time we set off for home. Then Dad took a wrong turn and we got lost in the dark. It was near midnight before he found the right track. He knew that Mom would be worried about us so he drove like a rally driver all the way back to Twilight.

We were just slowing down as we came up towards the old Home when one of the tires blew out with a bang. The car slewed to the left, side-swiped a tree, and skidded head-on into a post in Eddy Benson's boundary fence. The engine stalled and the lights went out. Our seat belts held us so we weren't hurt, but the front of the car was a mess.

Dad was shocked and mad. "Blast!" he said.

We both stood beside the car for a minute, but there was nothing we could do about it.

"We'll have to leave the thing here and walk home," Dad said. "Do you feel up to it?"

"Yeah. I'm okay."

As we started to walk back towards the road I looked up at the old Home and suddenly stopped. The skin on the back of my neck started to creep.

Someone was watching us from the entrance. It was the figure of a girl about thirteen or fourteen years old. She was wearing a filmy white dress.

About Colin Thiele

When I was twelve years old I had to leave home and stay with two old uncles in a town called Eudunda in order to go to secondary school there.

After dinner at night my uncles would sit in front of the fire and tell ghost stories. For the first week or so I was almost too scared to go to my room afterwards, in case a ghoulie was hiding under the bed. But after a while I decided that most of the stories were just good stories and I started to enjoy them.

I soon found out that many other people also liked ghost stories. So here is another one. It isn't one of my uncles', but one I made up myself. I often like to leave things unsolved at the end of a story so that we can't quite decide whether the ghost in it really existed. *The Twilight Ghost* is like that.